wednesday

anne bertier

ENCHANTED LION BOOKS

NEW YORK

Every Wednesday, Little Round and Big Square

get together to play their favorite game.

As soon as one of them says a word,

they transform themselves into it.

"Hurry up, Big Square! It's your turn to begin."

"Butterfly!"

"I'm a butterfly, too!"

"Mushroom!"

"Mushroom!!!"

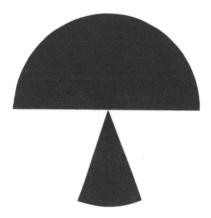

"Look, Little Round, look! Fence!"

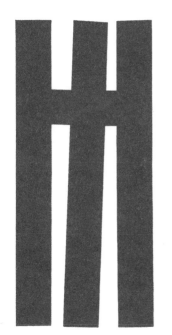

"Kite!"

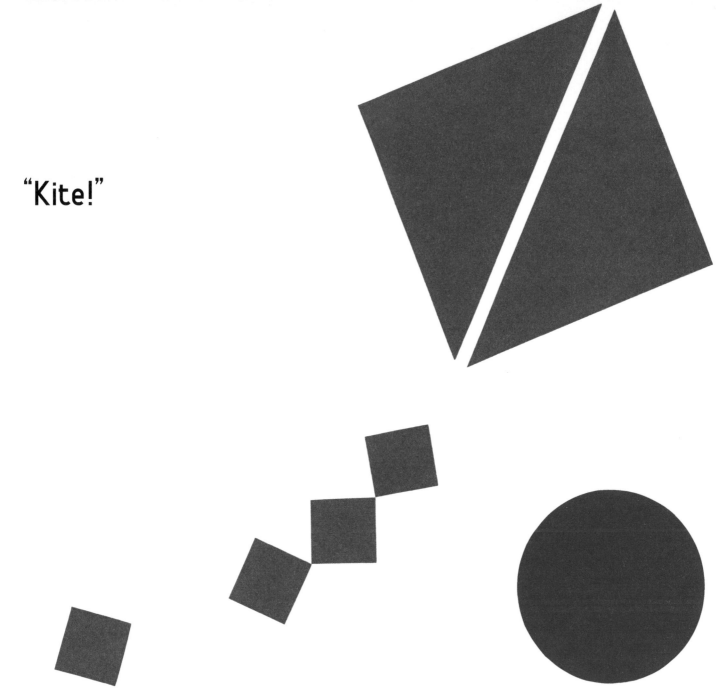

"I can't do that," sighs Little Round. "I'm too little."

"Pine tree, house!"

"Stop, Big Square, I can't do it!"

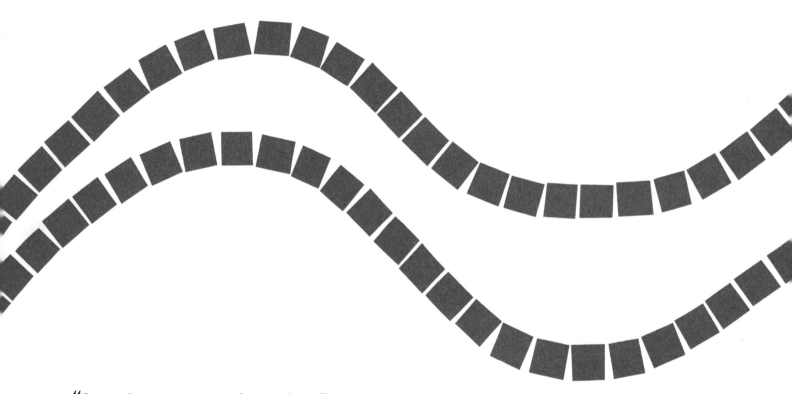

"Look at me, Little Round,

I'm the color of the sky and the sea!

It's so great! I'm waves and mountains."

"You're showing off.

I'm not playing anymore."

Each goes into its own corner.

But in an instant, Little Round says:

"What if both of us think of things together?"

"That's a good idea, Little Round. Let's try it right now."

"I'm going to hold myself very tall and straight."

"And I'll be the dot," says Little Round.

"Our i really works!"

"I'm going to stay round," Little Round decides.

"And me, let me see...

Snap, snap, snap! Surprise!"

"Awesome! A candy!"

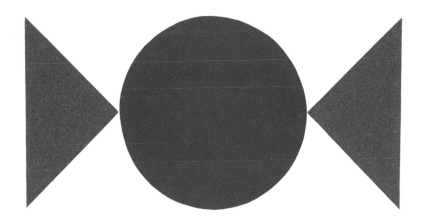

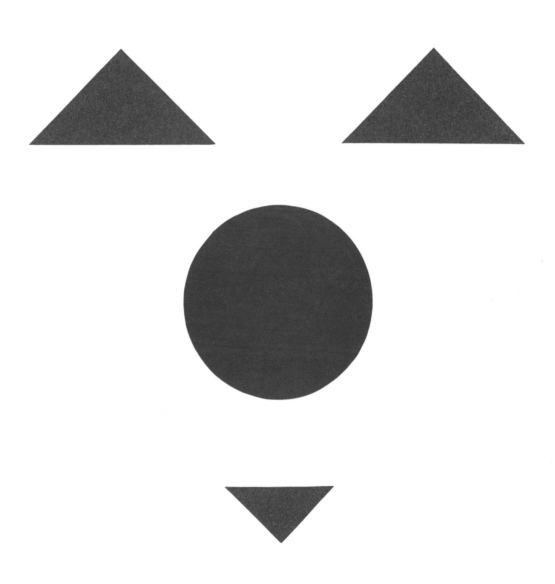

"A clown!"

"This is incredible!

We're a hat, a boat, a bowl! This is so great!"

Little Round and Big Square shout with joy.

Little Round becomes cheeks,

wheels.

Big Square becomes a hat and a coat.

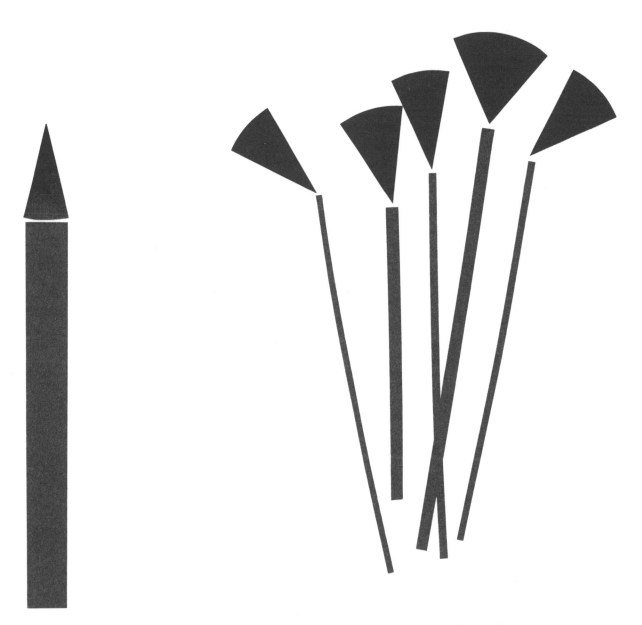

Together they become a pencil and a bouquet.

Sometimes they make

strange things...

...that then take shape.

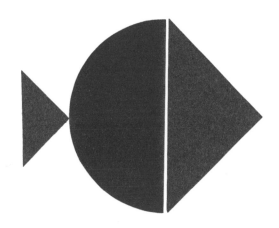

"All of this activity has made me hungry!

Let's make a snack, Little Round."

Together they shout:

"baker, pan, spoon, rolling pin!"

"Ice cream!"

The treats are so good that

our friends don't say another word.

They savor their beautiful afternoon.

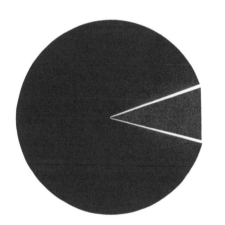

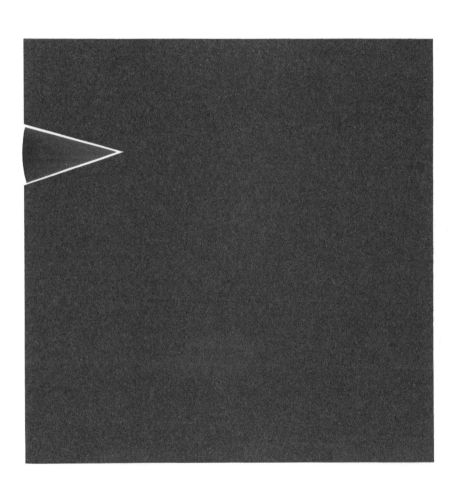

With thanks to Philip Nel for inspiring me to act! CZB

First American edition published in 2014 by Enchanted Lion Books
351 Van Brunt Street, Brooklyn, NY 11231
Translation Copyright © 2014 by Enchanted Lion Books
Translated from the French by Claudia Z. Bedrick
Originally published in France by Éditions MeMo, Copyright © 2010 as **Mercredi**
All rights reserved under International and Pan−American Copyright Conventions
A CIP record is on file with the Library of Congress ISBN 978−1−59270−152−0
Printed in March 2014 by PBtisk, Czech Republic, on paper from sustainably−managed forests

31901055637435